BUILDING SHOWJUMPING COURSES

A Guide for Beginners

MAUREEN SUMMERS

The Pony Club

First published in 2008
by The Pony Club
Stoneleigh Park
Kenilworth
Warwickshire CV8 2RW

© 2008 *Text and photographs* Maureen Summers
Publishing Consultant Barbara Cooper
Designer Nancy Lawrence

ISBN 978-09553374-5-1

British Library Cataloguing in Publication Data available on request

Printed in England by Halstan & Co Ltd, Amersham

Author's Acknowledgements

My thanks are due to Gatcombe Horse Trials for permission to use photographs
on pages 10, 11, 12, 13, 15, 21, 22, 23, 24, 28, 29, 31, 44, 45, 46.
Lynne Benfiled for flower decoration pages 15, 21, 23, 24, 31.
David Ackland for computerising the course plans on pages 37, 48, 49, 50.
Last but not least my daughter Justine for turning my almost
unreadable long hand into something more reader-friendly.

CONTENTS

INTRODUCTION

Many years ago, when my children were small and on ponies, we were members of the Kingshill Riding Club. This was a very small affair, with its own field on a very steep slope, with an awful old caravan as the judges' box, which eventually collapsed and blew away. Horses and ponies went in all classes.

I built the courses here for several years, with very little knowledge, but I learnt so much from just watching how everything rode. I learned about distances, the types of turns horses/ponies could cope with, going up and down hills, and much more.

Building a safe and jumpable show jumping course requires an awareness of many factors. It is important to be able to assess the size and stride lengths of the animals involved, the level of experience of the horses and /or riders, the terrain, the size of the arena, and the safe utilization of the materials that are available.

Where horses and ponies are competing together, as often happens in Pony Club competitions, the problems of building fair distances are obviously magnified. The aim of this book is to help, advise, and suggest how these problems can be overcome; it offers easy-to-follow guidelines as well as charts to help with distances in double and treble combinations.

It is said that an experienced rider can cope with any course whereas a novice rider needs a good course to encourage and improve him. I hope that this book will help the amateur course builder to understand that there is more to course building than just putting up a few jumps. Although it is not rocket science, it does take plenty of thought, and there should be a reason for everything that you do – even if it is only a common sense one.

It will be important for you to watch the competitors over the course you have created. Don't just build it and turn your back. Never be afraid to alter something for the next class if it is not working as you would wish. Listen to riders' comments as they walk the course, and sift out what could be relevant, rather than what they would prefer for their own ends. You will make mistakes - hopefully not too many or too great – but you will learn from them.

Always remember that, particularly in novice competitions, you can stop a horse far more quickly than you can start it again.

For further experience, help a qualified course builder but choose a show which has basic low level novice classes. These will be the types of courses that you will need for your use, particularly if you are building for Pony Club competitions.

Course building *is* hard work, but it can be eased with careful planning – and it is so rewarding when you watch a good horse jumping a lovely round over a course which *you* have invented.

I do hope that this will help and encourage you to design good courses, and that the sun will shine while you are building them.

Maureen Summers
Gloucestershire
2008

SECTION 1
Building Individual Fences

A course is made up of jumps of different types, materials and dimensions. Before considering the actual design of the course itself, it is worth taking a look at the materials that will be available to set it up, the different ways in which the various components may be used, and to what ends.

THE SHAPE

There are 4 basic shapes of jump

A Vertical or Upright
B Ascending Oxer or Parallel
C Square Oxer or Parallel
D Staircase

A. Vertical

The vertical jump consists of one pair of wingstands, with poles and fillers in the same vertical plane. Gates, planks and walls - which some riders find hardest to judge come into this category. Accuracy is needed when riding this type of jump.

Fig. 1 Two examples of true upright, or vertical, fences

Verticals can be made easier in novice classes by the careful placement of walls/brushes etc. underneath the poles. The following four illustrations show how this may be achieved:

1. Easiest. A filler set in front of the jump will help the horse to make a more rounded, natural jump.

2. Easier.

3. True vertical.

4. False groundline and totally illegal. Must never be used under any circumstances because the horse's eye will be assessing where the base of the jump will be, and a false groundline sets a trap which is not acceptable.

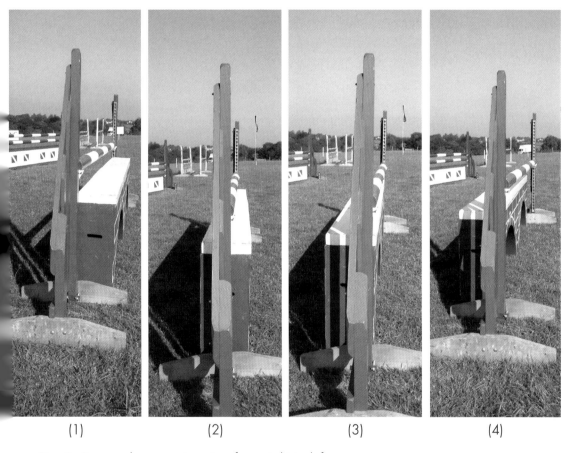

(1)   (2)   (3)   (4)

Fig. 2 Fences shown as jumping from right to left.

B. Ascending Oxer

This jump consists of two pairs of wingstands, with the front pole lower than the back, enabling the horse to see exactly what he is expected to jump; it is arguably the easiest of all jumps. Again, help can be given to the novice rider by pulling forward the filler. The lower the front pole the easier the fence becomes.

Fig. 3 Ascending oxer.

C. Square Oxer

Two pairs of wingstands, but with top poles of the same height. This jump is possibly the most difficult, and a degree of accuracy is required by the rider, as obviously the back bar has to be reached, (but not at the expense of knocking the front bar in the process).

Great care is needed in building a square oxer, particularly going downhill, as the back pole must be seen; it must appear no lower than the front, so as not to spring a nasty surprise on the horse.

Fig. 4 Square oxer.

D. Staircase

The staircase usually consists of three pairs of wingstands, with the poles becoming progressively higher. A small wall or brush can replace the lower pole, and an extra pole can be placed under the centre pole, depending on how solid the designer wishes it to look.

A convex triple bar is easier to jump than one that is flat, as it encourages a rounded jump, but a concave one must never be used. The best way to make sure that it is right is to lay your ruler across the three bars. If the middle bar does not touch the ruler, it is concave. If it touches it, it is flat, and if the ruler rocks on the middle bar, it is convex.

This fence is an interesting addition to a course, as long as there is enough material to build it. Firstly, it is different - obviously - and makes a nice visual effect for the spectators. Secondly, it is not often used, so is of added interest for the riders. As it is wider, some riders tend to attack it, but this is unnecessary, as the horse would be clearing the height of the lower bar even if it were not there at all. The idea is to present the horse as close as possible to the base of the jump, keeping in the same rhythm.

In higher grades of competition a triple bar is sometimes followed, in a related distance (of which more later) by an upright, testing the rider's control of his mount.

A triple bar should **never be used after a two stride distance in any combination:** the reason being that a long striding horse might put in only one stride but because the width of a triple bar is greater than a normal spread fence the back bar could be too far for the horse to clear. Although not a rule, for safety purposes the novice course builder would be advised not to use triple bars in any combination.

Fig. 5 Making sure that a staircase fence has been built correctly.

Fig. 6 A well-built staircase triple bar, dressed with flowers and ready for
a competition.

Fig. 7 A square oxer with small walls and pillars. Note also the correctly positioned flags. *Mediterranean Games, Athens 1991*.

THE FRAME

Not every show will have a standard set of B.S.J.A. jumps available. The following include other types that may be supplied, with guidelines on how best to use them.

Wingstands

Standard wingstands are probably the easiest to use. A pair is made up of a left and a right. The middle slats can be seen, (from the front), to be fixed to the cross bars at the back, with all bolt ends to the front and the sharp edges of the nut away from the approaching horse, for safety purposes.

Wingstands have detachable feet for convenient transporting and storage; they will have to be put on before you build your course. It is useful to have a spanner handy to tighten the nuts if they have become rusted, otherwise the wings will become more and more floppy as the day goes on, and in doing so can alter the spread on a jump.

If there is a shortage of wingstands, jump stands are useful for the back of spread fences, but never put them in front of wings, as this will encourage the horse to run out.

Some sets of fences have pillars, which make the course more attractive for the spectator. Some pillars have holes for the jump cups, and some simply stand at the end of a wall, for decoration. Never stand a pair of pillars behind a pair of wingstands to make an oxer. If you wish to have two pairs of pillars (as in fig.7), safety cups must be used for the back pole.

JUMP CUPS

The cups are an important part of the jump. Nowadays in B.S.J.A. sets of jumps the cups are made of plastic. Each wingstand is fitted with a metal strip with holes into which the cups slide.

For safety reasons, a holder has been designed for the back poles of spread fences, into which the cup is inserted. This releases the cup should a horse land on the back pole, which in the past has been a cause of back problems in the horse. It is a rule that this type of cup must be used on the back.

The plastic cups are curved at the top to hold the poles, but flat on the bottom, so must be turned upside down for use with planks, gates and hanging fillers.

Fig. 8 A standard jump-cup.

14

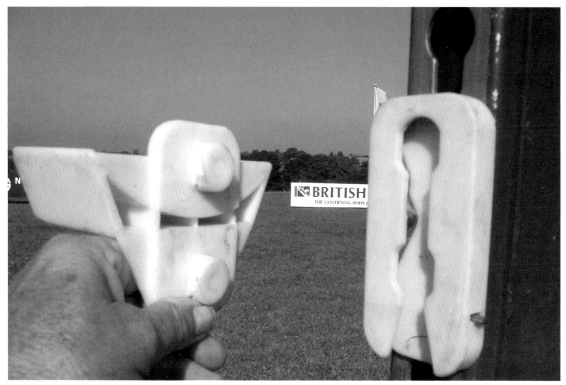

Fig. 9 Fitting a cup correctly into a safety-holder at the back of a spread fence.

Fig.10 Positioning of planks:
correct (top) on flat
side of cup;
incorrect (below) on
curved side of cup.

Metal Jump Cups

Some sets of fences still have the old-fashioned metal cups. It is important to remember that there are two different types: round ones for poles and flat ones for planks, gates, hanging fillers, etc.

If you are using these it is important never to put pillars on the back of spread fences, as they would be very unforgiving should a horse come down on the back pole.

It is wise, but not a rule, to put the pin through the wing from the front of the obstacle. In this way, should a horse refuse and lean on the jump - knocking it over - the cup will not fall out.

Fig. 11 The two types of metal cup.

POLES

Poles are generally 12 - foot (3.65m) long and are painted in different colours. However using a mix of colours in one fence is messy and unsightly.

Sometimes some rustic poles are supplied, and these can make a less daunting first fence in a novice competition.

Narrow poles (stile) usually 8 - foot long, can make a difficult fence, as optically they will seem higher than the rest of the course.

Fig. 12 A narrow fence, or 'stile'.

FILLING-IN MATERIALS

Fillers are an important part of the make-up of a jump. They are not used solely for visual effect, although this is important. How you use the material will determine the degree of difficulty of the jump. We have already discussed the placement of standing fillers: i.e. walls, brushes, hurdles etc. and how the horse/rider combination can be helped or tested with a forward or centrally placed groundline. The height of the filler and how the poles are spaced will also play an important part. For example a solidly built fence will encourage bold, confident jumping, whereas a gappy, more open jump is not so imposing to the horse's eye, and will need skill on the part of the rider to negotiate it carefully.

Hanging Panel

Probably the most common filler is the hanging panel, which must be placed on flat cups.

Fig. 13 A hanging panel. Due to a high wind blowing the panel down at the time this was photographed the flat cups had been replaced with curved ones.

18

Small Walls

The small wall is most useful - as, being free standing, it can be placed where you want it, and there are many types. A plain 2-foot wall is the one most used, but viaduct walls and arch walls always seem to pose a different problem: horses seem to be suspicious of something lurking in their depths.

A small wall 1-foot or 1-foot 6 inches high is very useful in making a jump look attractive.

Ladders

Ladders are in most sets of obstacles, but must never be used as the top element of a jump. At least one pole must always be above it. They are usually 1 foot and 2 foot high, and the smaller ones can mix and match with walls to make an extremely attractive jump.

Fig. 14 A ladder and wall together, making an attractive fence.

Planks

Planks can also be incorporated into other jumps.

Brush Fences

Brush fences are useful, as they are also free standing. They come in different heights. A water jump brush is set at a sloping angle to encourage the horse over the water, but this can also be used in other jumps, particularly at the base of a triple bar.

Water Tray

If a water tray has been provided you must check the rules of the competition to make sure that you are allowed to use it. It makes an

Fig. 15 A water tray.

interesting addition to the course, as again it has a different visual aspect. Parallel bars can be built over it as in the illustration, or it can be placed under the centre of an upright. It can be built with a small ladder in front and 3 poles behind at the back, making it a 'Liverpool'. This is virtually a staircase fence, and will need safety cups on **all** the back poles.

If the set is not a standard one and is lacking in infill materials there is plenty of room for improvisation. If, however, the material is not purpose-built, the utmost care must be taken to make sure that it is safe.

Straw Bales make ideal fillers, but the string must be absolutely tight, so that a horse cannot get his hoof through it.

Barrels are also useful, but they should be secured on either side by a pole, held by pegs, to prevent them rolling. They must be sound, and not rusty, so that a horse cannot put his hoof through them.

Fig. 15a Liverpool Jump

21

SECTION 2
Safety

This is the most important factor in the building of any course. Every precaution must be taken to ensure that the horse is not hurt in any way. There are many points that must be made in this section, some of which will have already been mentioned, but repetition will do no harm in this case.

1. When placing the pole in the cup make sure that there is room for your hand between the end of the pole and the wingstand. This will ensure that the pole will not become wedged – effectively turning it into a fixed fence.

2. Make sure that all the poles, planks etc. are on the correct cups, as already explained in the cup section.

3. Always make sure that there is a pole above a hanging filler. Panels and ladders must never be the top element.

4. Only a single pole is permitted on the back of a spread fence. Never put a pole under the back pole, and never put a plank or hanging filler on the back.

The only time when more than one pole is permissible is on a 'Liverpool', where the front is extremely low and all back poles are visible. If you decide to use this type of fence the back poles must have plenty of space between them, and must all be in safety cups.

5. If using a full-sized gate which is too high for the class for which you are building, never lean it to reduce its height, as it will become wedged in the cups and will in effect be a fixed fence.

6. Be careful when using pillars. As already mentioned, they must not be put on the back of a spread if using old metal cups, and never behind wingstands.

7. On windy days, gates and hanging fillers are liable to swing, sometimes with the base going away from the horse, making a false groundline. It is useful to have several wooden pegs in the boot of your car, which can be knocked into the ground to prevent this.

8. If you are using barrels they should also be pegged. Place a pole along either side of the row of barrels to hold them, and peg the poles. This stops them rolling about if pushed by a horse refusing and sliding into them, and ensures that they are always maintained in the same position.

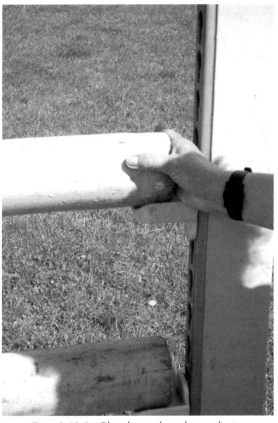

Fig. 16(a) Checking that the pole is not wedged against the wing.

Fig. 16(b) Wooden peg positioned to prevent gate from swinging.

9. One of the most common faults of unaffiliated course building is the placement of a loose pole at the bottom of a fence. A refusing horse can put a foot on this, whereupon it will slide away, possibly causing a tendon injury. If the holes in the wing don't go as low as you want them to, either peg the pole, or, as in Fig 18 drop the pole into a pair of brush feet.

10. If you wish to leave spare cups at a jump in readiness for the height to be increased in the later competitions, make sure that they are tucked away safely where a loose rider cannot land on them.

11. In all jumps which are held together with bolts: i.e. planks, gates etc., the bolt head must be on the face of the jump, and towards the oncoming horse, with the protruding nuts on the reverse side.

12. The final safety aspect involves the striding in double and treble combinations, and the type of jumps used therein, and also related distances. As this is such a vital issue, particularly when building for Pony Club competitions – when anything from a 16 hand horse down to a 12.2 pony, with all their varying strides may be in the same class – there is a separate section on this subject.

Fig. 17 This illustrates the common but dangerous practice of placing a pole on the ground at the base of a fence. It is not allowed in competitions.

Fig. 18 A brush foot and its simple use as a safety device.

SECTION 3
Double and Treble Combinations

Combinations consist of two or three jumps in a straight line with either one or two non-jumping strides between them. This in itself is a test of the training of the horse, and the course designer should never add extra difficulty by putting, through a treble, a long distance to a short one, and vice versa. It would completely upset the flow of the course to have a pull/kick on, or a kick/pull situation.

The tables which follow act as a guide to the basic distances between fences, but many factors affect the horse's stride, and the conditions of the day have to be taken into consideration: i.e. a horse's stride will shorten by up to 1 foot (30cm) if:

(a) It is muddy.
(b) The going is uphill.
(c) If is a confined jumping arena.
(d) If it is going away from home.

Where these conditions prevail, use the shorter distances in the table.

Likewise, the horse will lengthen his stride by up to 1 foot (30cm) if:

(a) The going is springy.
(b) There is a gentle downhill slope (steep slopes tend to make the horse 'prop' or steady himself).
(c) It is a large open arena.
(d) If he is heading towards home.

If the jumps are lower than 3 feet (90cm), shorten the distance slightly so that the horse is not encouraged to jump long and flat.

It is essential to have a measuring tape for setting up combinations accurately. The distance should be measured from the *back* of the front element to the *front* of the next, measuring the distance at both ends of the poles.

Make sure that the jumps are in a straight line. In outside arenas it is easiest to do this by standing at the front and looking down the centre colour of the poles. Indoors, a cabbage line can be laid down and the outside foot of each wing placed at right angles against it. This doesn't work outside, as even a flat looking field is seldom what it seems, and the slightest mound will tilt wings in the wrong direction, throwing the poles out of alignment.

As shown in fig. 19. a combination looks at its best if it is of the same colours throughout. Not only does it tell the spectator that is all one jump, but it is easier for the horse not to have a muddle of colours. It is important, particularly in novice competitions, to have the largest, most obvious filler at the first element; it gives the horse something to focus on. If it is further on in the combination, it could take the eye of the horse, preventing him from concentrating on the first part and jumping correctly.

The easiest jump into a combination is an attractive ascending spread. Anything too startling, or a very upright fence, will back the horse off, and cause him to land more steeply than he should, which will make him have to reach for the next stride, or put in an extra one.

If a combination is in a plain colour - i.e. rustic – it is easier to first build it with coloured top poles – to obtain a straight line.

Fig. 19 Combination fence, colour co-ordinated, designed for the C.I.C. at Gatcombe Horse Trials.

CHART A: ONE NON-JUMPING STRIDE

N.B. These are guidelines only and should be adapted to your own circumstances

(v) = Vertical (sq) = Square Oxer (as) = Ascending Spread

	(v) (v)	(v) (sq)	(v) (as)
Horses over 14.2	7.30m - 7.90m (24' - 26')	7.15m - 7.60m (23' 6" - 25')	7m - 7.60m (23' - 25')
14.2	6.85m - 7.45m (22' 6" - 24' 6")	6.55m - 7.15m (21' 6" - 23' 6")	6.55m - 7.15m (21' 6" - 23' 6")
13.2	6.40m - 7.00m (21' - 23 ')	NOT USED	NOT USED
12.2	6.10m - 6.70m (20' - 22')	NOT USED	NOT USED

	(sq) (v)	(sq) (sq)	(sq) (as)
Horses over 14.2	7.45m - 7.75m (24' 6" - 25' 6")	7.00m - 7.30m (23' - 24')	6.85m - 7.30m (22' 6" - 24')
14.2	6.70m - 7.30m (22' - 24')	NOT USED	NOT USED
13.2	6.40m - 7.00m (21' - 23')	NOT USED	NOT USED
12.2	6.10m - 6.70m (20' - 22')	NOT USED	NOT USED

	(as) (v)	(as) (sq)	(as) (as)
Horses over 14.2	7.45m - 7.90m (24' 6" - 26')	7.00m - 7.45m (23' - 24' 6")	7.00m - 7.45m (23' - 24' 6")
14.2	6.70m - 7.30m (22' - 24')	NOT USED	NOT USED
13.2	6.40m - 7.00m (21' - 23')	NOT USED	NOT USED
12.2	6.10m - 6.70m (20' - 22')	NOT USED	NOT USED

CHART B: TWO NON-JUMPING STRIDES

N.B. These are guidelines only and should be adapted to your own circumstances

(v) = Vertical   (sq) = Square Oxer   (as) = Ascending Spread

	|→| (v) (v)	|→|| (v) (sq)	|→|| (v) (as)
Horses over 14.2	10.50m - 10.95m (34' 6" - 36')	10.50m - 10.80m (34' 6"- 35' 6")	10.35m - 10.80m (34' - 35' 6")
14.2	9.75m - 10.65m (32' - 35')	9.75m - 10.05m (32' - 33')	9.60m - 10.20m (31' 6" - 33' 6")
13.2	9.45m - 10.05m (31' - 33 ')	9.15m - 9.75m (30' - 32')	9.15m - 9.90m (30' - 32' 6")
12.2	9.00m – 9.60m (29' 6" - 31' 6")	8.85m – 9.45m (29' - 31')	8.85m – 9.45m (29' - 31')

	||→| (sq) (v)	||→|| (sq) (sq)	||→|| (sq) (as)
Horses over 14.2	10.50m - 10.80m (34' 6" - 35' 6")	10.35m - 10.65m (34' - 35')	10.00m - 10.65m (33' - 35')
14.2	9.75m - 10.35m (32' - 34')	9.60m - 10.20m (31' 6" - 33' 6")	9.60m - 10.20m (31' 6" - 33' 6")
13.2	9.15m - 9.90m (30' - 32' 6")	9.00m - 9.75m (29' 6" - 32')	9.15m - 9.90m (30' - 32' 6")
12.2	8.85m - 9.30m (29' - 30' 6")	NOT USED	NOT USED

	||→| (as) (v)	||→|| (as) (sq)	||→|| (as) (as)
Horses over 14.2	10.50m - 10.95m (34' 6" - 36')	10.35m - 10.80m (34' - 35' 6")	10.20m - 10.80m (33' 6" - 35' 6")
14.2	9.90m - 10.65m (32' 6" - 35')	9.75m - 10.20m (32' - 33' 6")	9.60m - 10.20m (31' 6" - 33' 6")
13.2	9.30m - 9.90m (30' 6" - 32' 6")	9.15m - 9.75m (30' - 32')	9.15m - 9.75m (30' - 32')
12.2	8.85m - 9.45m (29' - 31')	NOT USED	NOT USED

SECTION 4
Related Distances

A related distance is the measured distance between two fences, to allow for three, four, or five non-jumping strides. Six strides can be measured, but it is such a long way that it is a waste of time.

With five - even four - non-jumping stride distances, the horse can be asked to lengthen and leave a stride out (particularly in jump-offs when time is a factor). Alternatively if he lands steeply over the first jump, or you want him to be more careful over the next he can be asked to shorten and put an extra stride in.

In classes for more experienced competitors the course designer can decide whether he wants to have a slightly longer or shorter distance to test the rider's ability and the horse's training, but again, as with combination fences, the condition of the day will dictate to a certain extent what is done.

CHART C:
A SMALL CHART TO HELP WITH RELATED DISTANCES

3 non - jumping strides	14.00m – 14.65m (46' – 48')
4 non - jumping strides	17.35m – 18.30m (57' – 60')
5 non - jumping strides	20.77m – 21.95m (68' – 72')

SECTION 5
Pony Club Competitions

You should obtain a current Pony Club rule book before starting to design courses for Pony Club classes, as each year minor changes might be made to the rules. Some of the basic everyday rules are included in this section.

In most Pony Club competitions there are horses and ponies of all shapes, sizes, and lengths of stride. It is totally impractical for the organisers to allow enough time for constant alterations to distances while the competition is taking place, so the problem must be addressed with this in mind.

It is a rule that combination fences (doubles or trebles) in any Pony Club competition, at any level, must be a minimum of five strides from the fence preceding it. This is so that the rider is not committed and can adapt his stride in readiness. Likewise, the fence following must be at least five strides away. If a horse/pony has a problem through the combination, it needs time to regroup, without being faced with another jump three or four strides later.

Horse distances *MUST* be built in these events. The more room a pony has to sort itself out the safer it is. It would be far easier for a 12.2hh pony to adapt to a horse distance than a 14.2hh distance, whereas a horse would be hard pushed to fit in a stride in a pony distance.

Horse distances will be too long for many of the smaller ponies. It is therefore a rule that if the course builder does decide to have a spread fence in double or treble combinations in any position other than the first element, it must be preceded by two non-jumping strides. It is preferable – particularly in minor competitions – for only an upright fence to be used as the second and third elements. If a pony has to put two strides in a horse one-stride distance, it will obviously be shortening his normal stride, and therefore probably slowing him down, which could prevent him from throwing his natural jump and if an oxer is used could land him on the back bar.

Later on there are two course plans: one simple and straightforward for the younger, or more novice element; the other showing a greater degree of difficulty. These may help to give you some ideas for your own use but it is important to bear in mind your own set of circumstances; i.e. size and shape of ring, position of entrance and exit etc. When in doubt, err on the side of simplicity. You will find that the very fact of riding in a competition, particularly in a team event, will bring the psychological aspect into play, and riders will make mistakes which otherwise they would not make. Nerves have had a lot to answer for in the past, as they will undoubtedly have in the future.

Fig. 20 How things were. Barnet Show, *circa* 1950.

Note the leaning gate and the 6-inch nails; also the standing martingale onto a drop noseband.

SECTION 6
Pre–planning the Course

Bearing in mind all the hints that have gone before, it is now time for you to draw up the course plans for the show.

It is very important that you spend some time at home pre-planning, looking at the schedule, and making yourself au fait with the rules of the competitions for which you are about to design. This includes:

- Number of jumps required
- Number of combination fences allowed, i.e. how many doubles and if a treble is included
- The maximum heights and spreads
- If there is a time limit
- If there is a jump-off

If there are several classes, or perhaps a team event with two different rounds, plan so that each course change is fairly quick and easy, with only a little moving of jumps, and maybe a reversal of one or two. No-one wants to watch exactly the same course jumped all day, but neither do they want to watch a course builder altering fences for any length of time.

It is important to have a good, flowing course, without tight difficult turns, and at least two changes of rein. Horses must be encouraged right from novice status to move forward freely and must not be asked to stop and start again which completely destroys the rhythm and balance, and also their confidence. You do not want to have a situation where the horse is asking 'do you want me to go or not?'

Ask the show secretary for the dimensions of the ring, the siting of the judges' box, and the position of the entrance and exit. If there is no timing equipment, try to place your start and finish in line with the judges' box, as this will help them to use their stop watches more accurately.

In novice classes remember to have at least the first jump, and if possible the second, going towards the collecting ring entrance, as this will help the more reluctant equine to get going. It is also useful to put the last jump in the region of the exit, as this will save time on the day should there be a large entry.

Mix spread fences with verticals to keep horse and rider alert.

Don't have your combination fences too early in the track. It is not advisable to put a double in before Number 4, with the treble combination later on and at least one individual fence between them. Also, for inexperienced horses, the first double going towards home is a help. Later on, for more experienced horses you can use the going away from home direction as one of your tests.

If you are building in a grass arena don't take the line of the jumping track through any combination fences; if it starts to rain the going will deteriorate as the class progresses and a carefully measured distance when the ground was dry will ride completely differently as the going deepens.

Jump-off

A jump-off should have at least six jumps (five indoors) including a double or treble. This becomes the most important aspect of the class, as from the jump-off comes the winner so if you cannot get a fluent design for this from your original first round plan, scrap it and start again.

It should be flowing, with one or two neat turns mixed with one or two straight runs, so that it doesn't favour any particular type of horse or pony.

You must put the order of jumps in the jump-off on your course plans, but they need not be in the same numerical order as in your first round. It is permissible to include an extra fence which has not been used in the first round if it helps you obtain a better track; this must be numbered and ready at the start of the competition, so that the riders can familiarize themselves with it as they walk the course, and it *must* be crossed off during the first round. It must conform to the class rules, and should not be built so that it springs a nasty surprise on the horse.

It is essential for any oxer in your jump-off not to be followed by a sharp turn back to another jump (a cut back). An inexperienced rider could land his mount on the back pole by trying to do a classy turn.

Rough Plans

When drawing your course plans it is important to show the judges' box along the bottom, wherever the entrance and exit are; as the judges will need a copy of any plan it will therefore be the correct way up for them to read.

Draw your rough plan on a large piece of paper: A4 is ideal. Use a pencil so that you can make alterations. Put arrows on each jump to denote the direction so put the number on the take-off side. Once you are happy with the route you can add lines for spreads.

Master Plan

Make a master plan for your own personal use and for any assistants that you may (or may not) have. This will include details of all your courses on the day, and the heights, spreads and distances of the first class that you will be building. You should use a different colour for each class, and apart from the first class, do **not** put any arrows in unless bringing in an additional obstacle later as this is the plan from which you will do the actual build and you will want to know in which direction to face it. Just make sure that the number is on the correct side for take-off. This will enable you to build your first course, as the only one arrowed, straight from the master plan.

When you have completed your master plan, encase it in a clear plastic folder to protect it from the weather, as this will be your work sheet for the day.

Remember the three main points of course building:

1. SAFETY

2. TO FIND THE CORRECT WINNER

3. TO ENTERTAIN THE SPECTATORS

Thoughts

Finally, make sure that you have designed the type of track suited to the classes in the schedule. Think of course-building as the springboard for producing the young horse or rider.

Really novice tracks should be like a nursery school for the horse; fun and games, and encouragement for the future.

Next stage up, a few more questions should be asked to prove that jumping is serious after all, to discover the amount of homework or training that has been done, and whether he has the obedience and concentration to put it all into practice in the strange environment of an arena.

Third stage – whether he really has the jumping ability required to go further: whether the rider himself can read our questions correctly and put the correct answers into practice with the partnership of his horse.

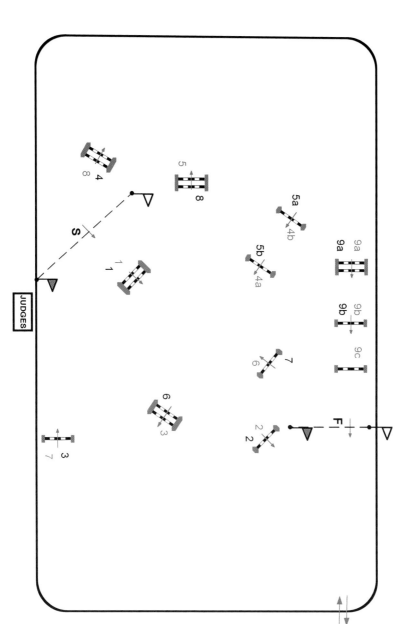

STROUD SHOW. DATE 1st MAY 2008

Class 1 Jump Off: 1, 3, 6, 7, 8, 9a, 9b.
Class 2 Jump Off, 2, 3, 4a, 5, 8, 9a, 9b, 9c

Fig. 21 Master plan showing the courses for two classes. Stroud Show 2008.

SECTION 7
Equipment

It must be pointed out that a certain amount of actual equipment will be needed. A measuring stick is a must; so is a measuring tape, as distances are too important to stride out and guess. Some competitions have a time allowed (after which time faults are incurred) and a time limit (twice the time allowed), after which comes elimination; this necessitates the measuring of the course with a proper measuring wheel, which is useful to own but expensive to buy. Your nearest B.S.J.A. course builder may be kind enough to lend you one if he is not using it at the time.

Most essential is waterproof gear. Flimsy shower-proof macs will not stand up to a day's torrential rain, and it is no fun after the day's jumping is finished to have to re-build for the next day if you are soaking wet and freezing cold. Wellington boots are good; even better are walking boots, as they are warm, waterproof and comfortable.

A box of tools in the boot of your car will be useful. Hammer and nails in case of breakages; a can of WD40 to loosen any rusty nuts on the feet; a spanner to tighten the feet when fitted to the wingstands; a mallet to knock gate pegs in; and the pegs themselves, plus brush feet which have already been mentioned.

Fig. 22 Equipment. Some items, such as tape and measuring-stick, are essential; others are not.

SECTION 8
Building the Course at the Show

It is usual to build the course the day before the show, and you will have arranged this with the secretary/organiser, who will have arranged for the set of jumps to be delivered to the site in readiness. If the jump wings have been transported without their feet, ask for a gang of helpers to fix them on, preferably before, or as you arrive, to save time.

The first thing you need to do is look at all the material that has been supplied, and decide what will be going where, making notes on your master plan. Try to vary the colours round the course (i.e. not all red in one corner) as it is more pleasing to the eye of the beholder. You may think that there won't be many spectators at minor shows, but there are always mums and dads and helpers, and it is nice if they enjoy it as well as the riders.

Don't make the mistake of building the jumps then discovering that they are in the wrong place and having to move them. This wastes time, energy and the bonhomie of any helpers so to avoid this start by putting a pole (of the right colour) down in the exact position that you think is right for each jump. It is much easier to adjust the angle of a pole than a complete jump.

Make sure that there is plenty of room at either end of the ring for the horses to turn, and that every jump has an open approach.

If you have two jumps fairly near to each other but further than a related distance, pace out the distance between them in multiples of four of your own (3ft/90cm) strides; this will ensure that the distance will ride on a fairly true stride. However still bear in mind the conditions of the day, which can affect stride lengths.

Try and be as adaptable as possible. If you have a fixed plan you will run into trouble if there is bad going, or a hole somewhere, or a tree perhaps.

When you have laid out your poles, stand back and ask yourself whether you could drive your car comfortably around the track. If you think this is possible, it should not present any difficulties for the competitors.

If you have a rule stipulating the maximum length of course: i.e. 450 metres, now is the time to measure it to make sure that you are within the maximum. Again, it is easier to make alterations at this juncture. Whilst you are measuring, your helpers could be moving the relevant material for each fence to the poles, including the cups. Leave a few spare poles neatly around the edge of the ring in case of breakages, or for when the heights of the jumps are put up in later classes.

Once everything is together, the frames can now be built, bearing in mind the height and spread required. While distances between jumps are measured from the back of the first one to the front of the next, the spread is measured differently. It is the overall width that is needed, so measure from the *front* of the front wingstand to the back of the *back* of the jump. Then you can put fillers in.

Give thought to how you want each fence to ride. Remember that poles placed close together (providing they are not too close to the cup above) will be easier to jump and more respected by the horse than a gappy fence. Square parallels are harder to jump than ascending ones.

If it is a qualifying competition, you will be expected to build up to the maximum height required (although not necessarily to the spread) but in minor competitions it is up to the course-builder to take into consideration the number of entries and their ability and experience (or lack of), and adjust accordingly.

If extra wingstands are needed later in the day they can be left neatly in pairs at the side of the ring. Don't leave them standing up, as they could get in the way of people sitting in cars. Don't put them in front of any banners should there be sponsors involved: this is not good P.R. at all.

If an upright is to become a spread later on, a spare pair of wingstands can be stowed away behind the ones in use, taking care not to place them where they might interfere with the fall of a pole.

- As stated before, spare cups can be safely tucked away behind the foot of the wingstand.

- Fence numbers should be placed in front of the right hand wing-stand.

- Flags, if used – red on the right, white on the left – should be placed at the face of each wingstand front and back (but not the middle of a triple bar) as near to the end of the poles as possible.

- The start and finish must be defined by flags, boards or markers. The distance from the start to the first fence is 6m (19' 8") – 25m (82') and from the last fence to the finish is 15m (49' 3") (6m indoors) – 25m.

When you have completely finished building the course, measure it once again walking it on the track that a careful rider would take. If in doubt about whether to go inside or around a particular jump, err on the side of caution. This now will give you a true instinct into how it will ride, as you will be seeing it in its entirety. If you are not happy with an angle, now is the time to make any last-minute adjustments.

Fig. 23 Wingstands stowed neatly at the ringside.

Fig. 24 Jump-cup left in a safe place for later use.

The final touch to the presentation of the course is decoration. Obviously it is outside the financial wherewithal of most minor shows to afford the services of professional 'flower people', but if you can manage to find some fir, and tie a branch or two to wingstands, it does make it more attractive. Don't make it too heavy, though, as if the ground gets muddy through the day, and you have to move jumps about a bit more than planned to give better going, you don't want to be too hampered by big trees and string.

It all seems a great deal to take in, but it soon becomes second nature, and you will learn a lot by watching how it is jumped by the various horses. See how it is riding, especially the distances, and be ready to tweak it if necessary for a following class if you think you may have misjudged something slightly.

Remember that you have to try and get a true result by building a fair course, using your judgment as to the use of heights, how you use fillers etc. A trappy course is *not* acceptable.

Fig.25 Spare wings, behind ones in use, ready for a later class requiring a spread fence.

Fig. 26(a) An un-decorated jump.

Fig. 26(b) The same jump after decoration.

Fig. 27 Measuring the height of a fence.

SECTION 9
Plans for Judges and Collecting Ring

Once your course is built and you are happy with it, your homework for that evening will be to do your course plans. Make them as neat and tidy as you possibly can. A course plan has to be supplied to the judges, and also to the collecting ring, where it should be displayed half an hour before the class.

The information required on the plan is as follows:

1. The name of the show, and date.

2. The number of class and title.

3. The position of the Judges' Box (at the base of the plan).

4. The Entrance and Exit to the ring.

5. The position of each jump; its number; and the direction in which it is jumped.

6. The lines of the Start and Finish.

7. If relevant, the length of course and speed required: i.e. 325mpm, the time limit and the time allowed (double the limit). To save time on calculations, a table of times and distances is included as an appendix.

Do **not** draw a continuous line around the track, as this denotes a compulsory route, deviation (i.e. passing the other side of a fence not in use for that class) from which would incur elimination. If you particularly wanted to cross your tracks, which normally would be faultable, a dotted line on the plan would permit this.

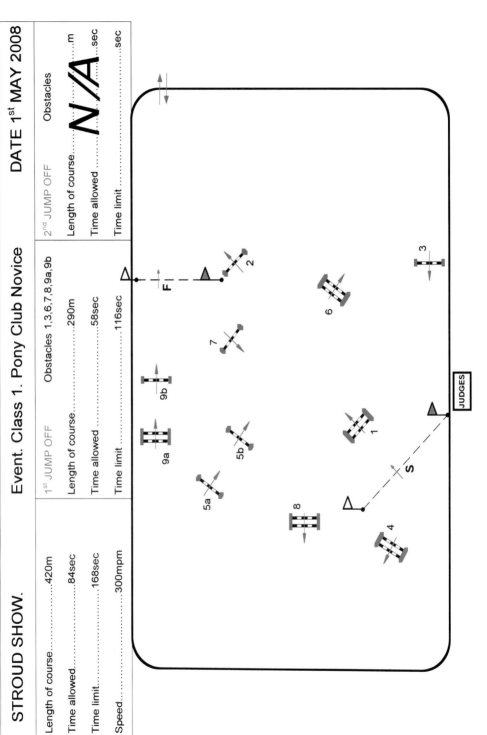

STROUD SHOW.

Event. Class 1. Pony Club Novice

DATE 1ˢᵗ MAY 2008

Length of course............420m	Obstacles 1,3,6,7,8,9a,9b
Time allowed...........84sec	
Time limit............168sec	
Speed..............300mpm	

1ˢᵗ JUMP OFF

Length of course.............290m

Time allowed............58sec

Time limit.............116sec

2ⁿᵈ JUMP OFF

Length of course..........N/A.........m

Time allowed............N/A.........sec

Time limit...........N/A.........sec

Fig. 28 Plan 1. A basic, straightforward course for Novices, with all the details required for the judges.

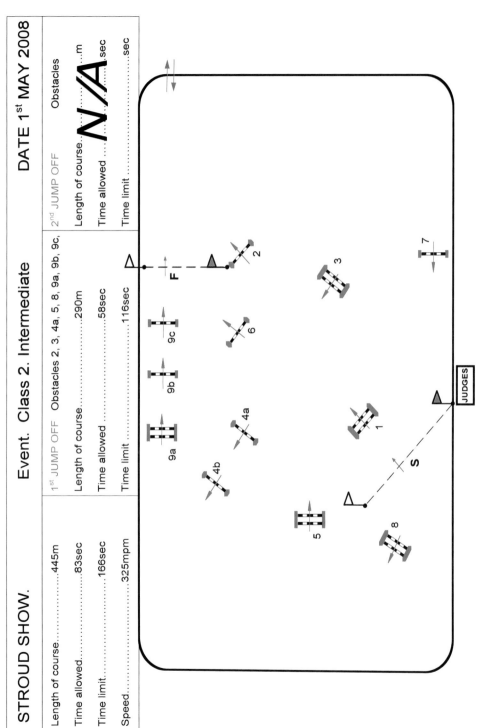

Fig. 29 Plan 2. Simple alterations to Plan 1, designed to produce a slightly more difficult course.

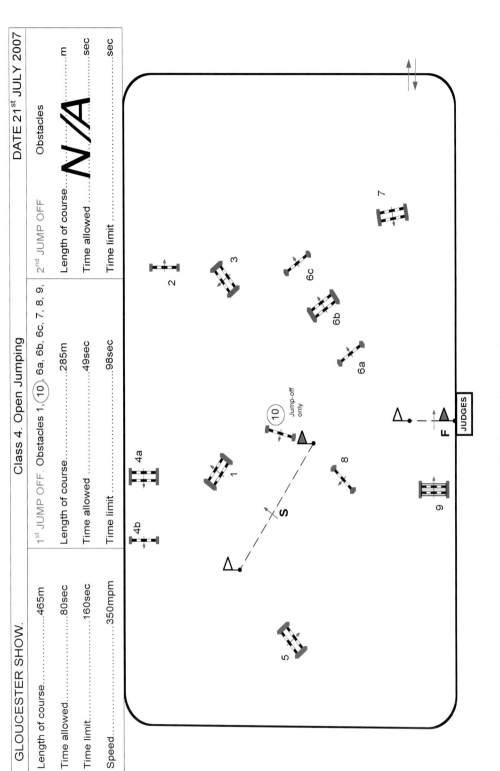

Fig. 30 Plan 3. This course is more technically demanding - with jumps on turns, and curves into other jumps. It has no connection with Plans 1 and 2.

SECTION 10
On the Day

Make sure you get to the showground in plenty of time on the day of the show, as you will have several tasks to perform:

1. The course plans must be supplied to the judges' box and the collecting ring.

2. It is well worth while going round your course with your measuring stick and checking everything. It is not unknown for heights to get mysteriously altered overnight, spreads to be narrowed, and wings to be kicked in, effectively preventing the poles from falling easily.

3. You will be expected to walk round the course with the judges, when they arrive. As they take responsibility for the course they obviously have to know exactly what it entails. If there are any queries as to why you have done something you are there to explain; and if they should want something altered it must be discussed with you and a good reason given for the alteration (e.g. wrong height, safety) to be made.

4. If the class is timed, stand behind the judges for the first five competitors to jump round without refusals, and check that the time is correct.

Arena Party

Before the horses start to jump you must brief your arena party:

• In the case of a knock-down they must not run out if the horse is likely to come back in their direction.

• If a horse stops at a jump and knocks it over in the process they must wait for the judge's bell before putting it back up, as this is what controls the rider. If the judge does **not** ring the bell – maybe he thinks the jump is still jumpable if only slightly disturbed – the rider will approach the fence again.

51

• They must check planks, gates and bricks on walls if knocked, even if they haven't fallen, as they may have been moved to the edge, making it unfair for the next competitor.

• Make sure that they know how the safety cups are put together, as, by their very nature, they will often come off during the course of the day.

• Sit them in pairs around the edge of the ring for safety, but not in front of any banners, (again bear in mind P.R.). Try to go over and chat to them during the day, and if the weather is hot make sure they have plenty to drink (non-alcoholic). Picking up poles all day can be quite soul-destroying, particularly if you are one small Boy Scout totally disinterested in horses, so explain a little about what is happening, to give them some interest. They are more likely to watch, and work hard if they are happy, and less likely to disappear.

• When the course is being altered for the jump-off or the next class, keep a careful eye on the height adjustment made by the inexperienced helper. A real muddle can occur if you tell someone to put the cup up two holes and they take it out, drop it, and forgetting where it came from, put it back at a totally different height from the other end of the pole.

• When you are not using a jump - i.e. in a jump-off, or the next class - it should be crossed off. If you have flags this is simple, as you take a red and a white flag from the front of the fence and just arrange them in a cross against the front of the jump. If there are no flags, one end of the top pole can be dropped to the ground (removing the empty cup for safety).

• Some people place the number from the right hand side of the jump to the centre. Do *not* take a pole and lie it across the top pole at right angles to it. This is dangerous, as the end of the pole will be quite high in the air and could be run into by a horse or a rider's face.

• If it is a one day show at the end of the day all the jumps must be taken down, feet removed, and stacked neatly for their transport to the next show. If there is more jumping on the next day after the last horse has jumped you will have to rebuild the course. This is another reason for you to have kept your course-changes fairly quick and simple through the day, as you will want to finish before darkness falls.

SECTION 11
Building Courses Indoors

You may be asked to build in an indoor arena, and although many of the previous hints in this book will apply, some will appear to be the exact opposite.

You will obviously have to know the exact dimensions of the school, and also the overall width of the jumps. With this knowledge and some graph paper you will be able to design a course to scale: which is important, as compared with an outdoor ring the area will seem very restricted.

Cut up some match sticks to the scale of the overall width of the jumps including the wingstands. These can be laid on your graph paper and moved about easily as you design your course. Alternatively, if you are computer literate it will be possible for you to transfer the necessary information on to your computer, enabling you to manipulate the fences to your design. You must make sure that all the fences have good visual approaches - i.e. that the horses will be able to see exactly what they are expected to jump. When you are sure of this you can then either draw up or print off your course plan and prepare your master plan.

The courses must be kept very straightforward, with extra attention given to the creation of easy turns. No jump must be nearer than 45' (13.50m) from each end of the school. You won't have to worry about weather conditions, hills, or ground problems, but you will have to take a lot of care with distances. There will have to be more related distances, as you won't have the space to get away from them, but the table shown in Chart C (page 30) can be safely used, as long as you lean towards the shorter distances.

If ponies are competing in the same class as horses, care will have to be taken as to where you place your spread fences.

If there is a time limit and you have to measure the course, be lenient, as it is difficult for horses to maintain a level speed in a restricted area.

For an indoor show it would be helpful if you were able to assist a qualified course builder before you worked by yourself. This will give you the general feel of building in a confined space, which really is a different ball game from out of doors.

Appendix

Time Allowed in seconds at various Speeds

Distances Metres	300m per minute	325m per minute	350m per minute
260	52	48	45
270	54	50	47
280	56	52	48
290	58	54	50
300	60	56	52
310	62	58	54
320	64	60	55
330	66	61	57
340	68	63	59
350	70	65	60
360	72	67	62
370	74	69	64
380	76	71	66
390	78	72	67
400	80	74	69
410	82	76	71
420	84	78	72
430	86	80	74
440	88	82	76
450	90	84	78
460	92	85	79
470	94	87	81
480	96	89	83
490	98	91	84
500	100	93	86
510	102	95	88
520	104	96	90
530	106	98	91
540	108	100	93
550	110	102	95
560	112	104	96
570	114	106	98
580	116	108	100
590	118	109	102
600	120	111	103

TWO EXAMPLES OF COURSE BUILDING AT ITS BEST

Fig. 31 *Mediterranean Games Athens 1991.*

INDEX